MOSES
Goes To School

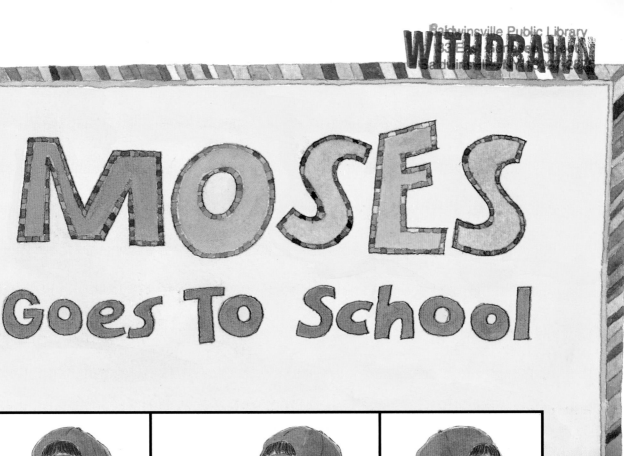

| I | GO TO | SCHOOL |

ISAAC MILLMAN

Frances Foster Books • Farrar, Straus and Giroux • New York

To Milo and Felix

Copyright © 2000 by Isaac Millman
Distributed in Canada by Douglas & McIntyre Ltd.
Color separations by Hong Kong Scanner Arts
Printed and bound in the United States of America by Berryville Graphics
First edition, 2000

Library of Congress Cataloging-in-Publication Data
Millman, Isaac.
    Moses goes to school / Isaac Millman. — 1st ed.
       p.   cm.
    "Frances Foster books."
    Summary: Moses and his friends enjoy the first day of school at their special school
for the deaf and hard of hearing, where they use sign language to talk to each other.
    ISBN 0-374-35069-8
    [1. Deaf—Fiction.   2. Hearing impaired—Fiction.   3. Physically handicapped—
Fiction.   4. Sign language—Fiction.   5. First day of school—Fiction.   6. Schools—
Fiction.]   I. Title.
PZ7.M63954Mp   2000
[E]—dc21   99-40582

AUTHOR'S NOTE

Children who are deaf and hard of hearing are very much like children who hear. They play with their friends, help their families, and sometimes misbehave. They take care of their pets and go to school. In school, they learn to read and write and use computers. They study science and arithmetic and learn about the world. They do sports, put on plays, sing songs, and go on class trips. Moses and his classmates communicate in American Sign Language, which is often called by its initials, ASL. ASL is a visual sign language composed of precise handshapes, movements, and facial expressions that are used to form words. Like any other language, ASL has its own grammar and syntax—its own way of putting a sentence together. For example, in ASL, "I love my dog" is signed "My dog [I] love."

I am grateful to Gail Gilson and the teachers at New York City's J.H.S. 47 School for the Deaf for letting me visit their classrooms. I thank Ashley Lockhart, a student at J.H.S. 47, for letting me use her letter and drawing of a dog. And I am indebted to Dorothy Cohler and Joel Goldfarb, Deaf teachers at the school, for the many, many hours they have spent helping me get the sign-language diagrams in my books right. If you follow carefully the position of the hands and fingers and the direction of the arrows shown in the diagrams, you can begin to learn a few words in American Sign Language.

HOW TO READ THE ARROWS AND SYMBOLS

Hand moves in direction of arrow

Right arc

Left arc

Slight wiggling motion

Writing motion

Swinging motion back and forth

On the first day of school, Moses and his classmates meet in the playground across the street from their school. It is a special school, a public school for the deaf. All the children are either deaf or hard of hearing. They communicate in sign language.

| I | GO TO | DEAF SCHOOL |

"Playtime is over, children," sign the teachers.
The children stop playing and line up with a partner. But they
don't stop signing. They haven't seen each other all summer and
they have a lot to say.
"My hamster gave birth to five tiny babies," Anna signs as she
pairs up with Dianne.
"I've got a cute new baby sister," Dianne signs. "She has no hair
on her head. She is bald."

A NEW   BABY   SISTER

"Look! I'm wearing new hearing aids," John signs.
"And I'm wearing new glasses," signs Moses.

MY   FRIEND   WEARS   HEARING AIDS

The school guards, Bernard and Jeannette, stop traffic so
the children and their teachers can safely cross the street.
The school guards are not deaf, but they know sign language.

The children find their assigned seats and chat while they wait for their teacher. "My aunt Josephine sent me a beautiful doll from Puerto Rico," signs Dianne.

"This summer we visited my Canadian cousins," signs John. "Now they're coming to visit us. They sent us a postcard with a beautiful stamp. I saved it for my stamp collection."

"I wrote a letter to my grandparents," signs Moses. "They live in France. Maybe I'll visit them next summer."

I

WROTE

A LETTER

Moses and his ten classmates stand when their teacher, Mr. Samuels, enters the classroom. Mr. Samuels wears hearing aids, too. "Good morning, children!" he signs.

"Good morning, Mr. Samuels!" the children sign in reply. Moses wonders why the teacher is bringing a large boom box to class.

IN CLASS WE STAND

In the morning, Moses and his classmates go next door to the Tech Room, where they work on their computer skills.

Then they practice their reading and writing. Since ASL is different from spoken English, they must learn to read and write English, as it is like another language.

"We will continue the morning lesson by writing to our pen pals," signs Mr. Samuels. Moses and his classmates compose their letters in ASL. They do it first on paper.

"Can we also send them our pictures?" Moses asks.

"Of course," replies Mr. Samuels.

The children photograph each other, using the school's digital camera. Mr. Samuels scans the picture Moses drew of his dog, Spot. Afterward, he transfers the images to the children's computers. Here is Moses' letter in ASL:

Dear Mark:

I'm moses and spot is my dog. I'm Happy Because play with dog. I'm love with dog. Why?
I can help teach the dog things. I teach for the play. How know this? We can Both play dog jump for Bone.

your friend
moses

Dear Mark,
I'm Moses and Spot is my dog.
I'm happy because I can play
with my dog. I love my dog.
Why? I can teach my dog different things.
We play together. How? He plays with
me and he jumps for his bone.

Your friend,
Moses

He types what he wrote on his computer. Then he makes
the changes that are needed to turn ASL into English. Mr.
Samuels helps him. When Moses has finished the letter, he
sends it by electronic mail to Mark at his school's Web site.
When Mark logs in on the Web site, using his password, he
will see that he has mail.

During their lunch break, Mr. Samuels has written the words to "Take Me Out to the Ball Game" on the blackboard. The children jump with joy. "A song, a song!" Now they know why Mr. Samuels brought a boom box to class.

I [AM]　HAPPY

Moses and his classmates don't hear the music, but they can feel the vibrations and sign the words to the song "Take Me Out to the Ball Game."

TAKE ME OUT   TO THE BALL GAME,

(Repeat: Take me out with the)   CROWD.   BUY

ME   SOME PEANUTS   AND

CRACKER JACK,

I DON'T CARE   IF I NEVER   GET BACK.

LET ME   ROOT, ROOT, ROOT   FOR THE HOME   TEAM,

IF   THEY   DON'T   WIN   IT'S A SHAME,

FOR IT'S   ONE   TWO   THREE

STRIKES,   YOU'RE OUT   AT THE OLD BALL GAME.

Afterward, they make a circle and dance.

The school day is over. The children put their books and pencils in their backpacks and say goodbye to the teacher.
"I'm glad you're our teacher, Mr. Samuels," signs Moses.

On the way out, Moses and his classmates say goodbye to
Jeannette and Bernard.
"Look at my new history book!" signs Dianne.
"We learned a song in class," signs Moses.
Bernard smiles. "Hurry, boys and girls, the bus driver is waiting."
"See you all tomorrow," Jeannette signs.

When the school bus stops in front of the apartment building
where Moses lives, his mother and his dog, Spot, are waiting.

I   LIVE IN   AN APARTMENT

Moses hugs his dog.

"How was the first day of school?" his mother asks as they wait for the elevator.

"Great, Mom!" signs Moses. "I have ten classmates. They come from many different countries, and all ten are my friends."

MY

DOG

3 | (snap fingers)

1　2

[I] LOVE

Moses unzips his backpack and shows his mother a picture,
which Mr. Samuels took, of Moses with his classmates.